TWO BEAR CUBS

TWO BEAR CUBS

A Miwok Legend from California's Yosemite Valley

Retold by Robert D. San Souci
Illustrated by Daniel San Souci

YOSEMITE ASSOCIATION
YOSEMITE NATIONAL PARK, CA

To the Ahwahneechee and all the other Miwok people
—R.S.S. & D.S.S.

Yosemite Association
P.O. Box 545
Yosemite National Park, CA 95389

The Yosemite Association is a non-profit, membership organization dedicated to the support of Yosemite National Park. Our publishing program is designed to provide an educational service and to increase the public's understanding of Yosemite's special qualities and needs. To learn more about our activities and other publications, or for information about membership, please write to the address above, or call (209) 379-2646.

 Library of Congress Cataloging-in-Publication Data
Two Bear Cubs
p.   cm.
Summary: Retells the Miwok Indian legend in which a little measuring worm saves two bear cubs stranded at the top of the rock known as El Capitan.
ISBN 0-939666-87-1
1. Miwok Indians—Folklore. 2. Legends—California—Yosemite Valley. [1. Miwok Indians—Folklore. 2. Indians of North America—California—Folklore. 3. Folklore—California.]
E99.M69T96   1997
398.2'097944704529757—dc21
[E]   97–17226
                                                     CIP
                                                      AC

The art for this book was created with watercolor paints on 140 pound cold pressed watercolor paper. It depicts the animal people of Ahwahnee in traditional Miwok garb, including buckskin skirts and loincloths, abalone shell and glass bead necklaces, and fur headbands.

Printed in Singapore. Third printing.

MANY SNOWS HAVE come and gone since this story was first told by the Miwok, whose name means "people" or "humans." They lived in the place they called *Ah-wah´-nee*, which is now known as Yosemite Valley. The Miwok believe that in the old days, the residents of *Ah-wah´-nee* were "animal people"– creatures that were part animal and part human.

ONCE, LONG AGO, Mother Grizzly Bear, *Oo-hoo´-mah-tee,* had two cubs she loved dearly. The first had sleek brown fur, just like her own. In those days, the young were not given names until they were nearly grown up. Because he had been born first, the brown cub was just called *Tah´-chee,* "Older Brother." The other cub, who had cinnamon-colored fur, was *Ee-tee-hoo´,* "Younger Brother."

One day the grizzly went to the river the old people named *Wa-kal´-la,* but which today is called the Merced. She took her cubs with her to catch rainbow trout and search for berries. However, the playful cubs waded into the water and splashed each other and scared away all the fish. Their mother gently scolded them, then sent them to hunt for berries.

So THE CUBS wandered along the riverbank, pausing to sniff the air for the scent of ripe raspberries. "Do not go far," Mother Grizzly had cautioned them. But the brothers forgot her warning as they raced, wrestled, played hide-and-seek, and threw stems of rattlesnake weed at one another. By the time they grew tired of this game, their fur was full of seeds.

They continued further and further downriver. When they grew hungry, they ate their fill of wild raspberries that they found. At last the cubs came to a spot where the river ran slow and shallow. From a huge boulder beside the stream, they dived into the water with terrific splashes. They paddled about and ducked one another and dove for pretty stones. They washed the seeds from their fur.

WEARY AT LAST, they scrambled up on the big flat rock and shook themselves. Then they lay down in the warm sunshine to dry off and nap. And as they dozed, the rock began to grow bigger and taller. For countless days and nights it continued to grow. The whole time, the two cubs slept on peacefully and never stirred as the rock rose higher and higher. When *Soo-you-k´*, Red-tailed Hawk, saw them so high in the blue heavens, he thought they would surely awake when the noon sun burned them. But the rock stopped growing long before it reached the sun.

While this was happening, Mother Grizzly discovered that her cubs were missing, and she began to search for them. She did not know that they now slept among the clouds. Tirelessly she searched through the passing seasons for her young.

IN HER WANDERING, the bear met *Yu´-wel*, Gray Fox, who was chipping arrowheads from bits of shiny black obsidian.

"Have you seen my cubs?" she asked.

"No," said Gray Fox, "but I will help you look for them."

Next, they asked *Tee-oo-week´*, Badger, who was pounding acorns with a stone, if she had seen the cubs.

"No," said Badger, "but I will help you seek them."

After this they went to the *u-ma-cha*, the cedar bark home, of *Oo-to-e´-ah*, Mother Deer.

"Have you seen my little ones?" Mother Grizzly asked the deer.

"No," replied Mother Deer, "but I will help you find them."

SOON THEY MET *He-le´-jah*, Mountain Lion, who was carrying a big bundle of firewood upon her back.

"Have you seen my cubs?" asked Mother Grizzly.

"No," said Mountain Lion. But she put down her firewood and joined the others in their search.

Lastly Mother Grizzly asked *Poo-see-nuh´*, little White-footed Mouse, "Have you seen my cubs?"

Mouse looked up from the basket she was weaving. She said, "No, but I will help you look for them."

Then the searchers looked everywhere a cub might be: in holes, in hollow logs, in thickets, and on tree branches. They sought the cubs where the tastiest wild plums and sweetest choke-cherries and the plants called "hummingbirds" that brimmed with nectar grew.

But they found no trace of the missing two.

Finally, the creatures sat together, trying to decide what they should do next.

SUDDENLY RED-TAILED HAWK swooped down. He called to the grieving Mother Grizzly, "I have seen your cubs. They are on the granite stone which has become a towering mountain."

Filled with wonder, the bear and her friends gathered at the base of what was now a wall of rock. They called and called, but the cubs slept on, too high to hear.

"Please fly up and help my children find their way down," Mother Grizzly begged Red-tailed Hawk.

So the hawk flew up toward the sleepers. But fierce winds blew around the stone that was now a mountain. The bird beat his wings, but he could not fight past the winds. At last he flew back down and said sadly to the grizzly, "I cannot reach your young ones."

THEN MOTHER GRIZZLY made a mighty leap up the wall. But she could find no purchase on the smooth stone, and so she tumbled back to earth. Again and again she tried. But in the end, she had to give up.

"Now who will save my cubs?" she wondered as she wept.

One by one the animals tried. Mouse tried jumping from stone to stone, but her heart grew faint when she was only a little distance up.

Clever Badger scrambled a bit higher before he reached a spot where he must leap from one ledge to another. Here his courage failed him.

THEN GRAY FOX and Mother Deer tried. Each got a little higher than the ones who had gone before, but neither reached even the halfway point.

Mountain Lion went farthest of all, climbing and leaping and climbing yet higher. On the ground below, Mother Grizzly's heart grew lighter. Surely the nimble lion would reach the cubs and guide them safely down to her.

But even the agile mountain lion reached a point where the rocky wall was too tall and steep. The smooth stone had no holds or outcroppings to help her climb higher. So she was forced to turn back.

"IS THERE NO one who can save my cubs?" asked poor Mother Grizzly.

"I will try," a small voice said. Looking down, the grizzly saw little Measuring Worm, *Tu-tok-a-na.*

All of the other animals laughed.

"Do you think you can do what Badger, Gray Fox, Mother Deer, and I myself have failed to do?" Mountain Lion challenged.

"Foolish Measuring Worm!" cried Mouse, "Your name is longer than you are."

But Mother Grizzly picked up the measuring worm and said gratefully, "I welcome your help."

So Measuring Worm began to creep up the rock, curling himself into an arch, anchoring himself with his four short back legs, then stretching out his body until his six front legs could grasp another bit of stone. Curling and stretching, he inched his way up. While he climbed, he chanted, *"Tu´-tok! Tu´-tok!"* When he curved his body, that was *"Tu´,"* and when he stretched out, that was *"tok."*

AS HE WENT, he marked the safe path with a sticky thread, for Measuring Worm can make a string like a spider.

In time, he went even higher than Mountain Lion. The animals below could no longer see him, or hear his little song, *"Tu´-tok! Tu´-tok!"*

Up and up and up he went. Day turned to night over and over, and still he climbed. Beneath him, Mother Grizzly and the other animals kept anxious watch. Above, the cubs slept peacefully, wrapped in cloud-blankets.

Once Measuring Worm looked down and saw that the mighty river now seemed only a thin band of silver, decorated with sparkling rapids and green islands. The forests and meadows of the valley floor looked no bigger than bunches of twigs and moss. At this sight, Measuring Worm grew afraid. For a time, he could not move at all. But he found his courage again. He began to sing, *"Tu´-tok! Tu´-tok!"* as loudly as he could, and crept still higher up the wall.

DAY AFTER DAY, Measuring Worm climbed, until at last, early one morning, he reached the top of the vast stone. He softly whispered into the ears of the two cubs, "Wake up!" He was afraid that if he woke them too quickly, they might become frightened and fall off the slippery rock.

When they saw how high above the river they were, the cubs began to cry. But Measuring Worm comforted them. "Follow me," he said. "I will guide you safely down the mountain, for I have marked a safe path with my string."

To the brown cub Measuring Worm said, "Older Brother, you follow right behind me." Then, to the one with cinnamon-colored fur, he said, "Younger Brother, follow your brother and make your every step the same as his. Do this, and you will not fall."

Still the cubs were fearful. But Measuring Worm said, "Surely Mother Grizzly's children are not cowards, for she is the bravest creature in *Ah-wah´-nee.*"

THEN THE TWO little bears puffed out their chests and said, "We are brave. We will follow you."

So they began the slow climb down, both cubs doing just what Measuring Worm told them.

After a long time, sharp-eyed Gray Fox spotted them. He told Mother Grizzly, "See! Your cubs are returning."

Anxiously she looked where her friend was pointing. Sure enough, there she saw her cubs making their way down the face of the mountain, as Measuring Worm guided their every step and called encouragement to them.

AT LAST THE little bears and their rescuer reached the valley floor. Then how joyfully Mother Grizzly gathered her cubs to her heart and hugged them and scolded them for not minding her and then hugged them again. Loudly she praised Measuring Worm for his courage and resourcefulness.

Then all the animals decided to call the rock that grew to be a mountain *Tu-tok-a-nu-la,* which means Measuring Worm Stone, in honor of the heroic worm who had done what no other creature could do. And so the towering landmark was known for many years, until newcomers renamed the huge granite wall, "El Capitan."

ABOUT THE LEGEND

This retelling is based on a traditional Southern Sierra Miwok tale, versions of which can be found in *Legends of the Yosemite Miwok*, compiled by Frank La Pena, Craig D. Bates, and Steven P. Medley; *Tribes of California*, by Stephen Powers; *Yosemite Indians*, by Elizabeth Godfrey; and *Californian Indian Nights' Entertainment*, compiled by Edward W. Gifford and Gwendoline Harris Block.

ABOUT THE MIWOK PEOPLE

Territory The people we call the Miwok were speakers of any one of seven distinct but related languages in Central California. Each of the language groups was made up of numerous, independent tribelets. The Coast Miwok lived north of San Francisco Bay, in what is now Marin County; the Bay Miwok resided in a section of Contra Costa County; the Lake Miwok occupied a portion of Lake County; the Plains Miwok were located in the Sacramento-San Joaquin delta region. The Northern, Central, and Southern Sierra Miwok occupied the Sierra Nevada foothills and mountains from El Dorado County south to Madera County. Yosemite Valley was home to some of the Southern Sierra Miwok.

Food The Sierra Miwok hunted deer and small game. Their diet also included a variety of plants, insects, and fish. They gathered mushrooms in the spring and fall, greens in spring, seeds in late summer and early fall, and acorns from the black oak—their most important food crop—in fall.

Women and children harvested acorns in late September or early October. They were placed first in winnowing baskets, then transferred to burden baskets to be carried home. The acorns would be set in the sun to dry, before being stored in a granary (*chuck-ah*) for later use. Prior to cooking, the acorns had to be cracked, the kernels cleaned of their inner skins, and the nuts pounded in a mortar. Next the pounded flour was sifted, then the fine flour was leached with water to rid it of the tannins that gave a bitter taste. The resulting dough was mixed with water in a cooking basket and boiled with hot stones to make mush.

Houses In the higher elevations, people lived in conical homes made of layers of incense cedar laid over a frame of tilted poles or in dome-shaped houses thatched with brush. Sweat lodges built of earth were used by men before hunting and for a variety of religious and healing ceremonies. Acorn granaries were constructed of upright poles and deerbrush bound with grapevines and thatched with conifer boughs to keep the rain out. The floor was usually two or three feet above the ground to prevent spoilage. A granary might hold five or six hundred pounds of acorns or other seed and nut crops.

Clothing and Appearance Animal skins provided the main source of clothing for the Miwok. Men wore loincloths of buckskin; women wore buckskin skirts. In winter, they kept warm by wrapping themselves in fur robes made from the tanned skins of larger animals, such as deer or mountain lion, or in blankets woven from strips of rabbit skin. Moccasins were worn in cold weather or on long journeys. Men and women wore their hair long—often to the waist—and sometimes had tattoos.

Until age two or so, babies were carried on their mothers' backs in cradle baskets woven from willow or other shoots. Children wore no clothes until age ten; they wrapped themselves in skins when the weather was cold. Their ears and noses (the septum) were pierced before they reached their teens. In their ears they wore flowers, shiny ear plugs of rubbed and charred pine, tubes of polished, hollow bird bones decorated with feathers, or earrings that were little strings of shells or beads. Nose sticks were usually made of polished bone or shell.

Boys and girls were occasionally tattooed, usually between the ages of twelve and fifteen. Designs covered the chin, shoulders, arms, hands, chest, stomach, and thighs. Cuts were made with sharp bits of obsidian; ashes were mixed with the drawn blood and rubbed into the thread-thin cuts.

Toys Toys included noisemakers and tops fashioned from acorns, whistles made from goose quills, bows and arrows for boys, and dolls created using shredded soaproot leaves for girls. Children played games like tag (several versions), hide-and-seek, and a guessing game in which someone had to guess in which hand another child had hidden a bit of charcoal.

Weapons and Tools The main weapon for hunting or making war was the bow and arrow. Bows were generally crafted from incense cedar or California nutmeg, with a string of twisted sinew or milkweed. Arrow shafts (usually syringa or wild rose) were feathered and tipped with obsidian points. These points were traded from Mono Lake Paiute people further to the east, or they were made locally from obsidian obtained in trade. Tools for chipping were made of deer antler, for sewing from deer bone, and for scraping from stone.

Baskets and Beads Basketry was a high art among the Miwok, practiced almost exclusively by women. Weavers used the young shoots of willow, redbud, and other shoots and roots as the raw materials. Each basket form was made for a specific purpose—carrying loads, harvesting grass seeds, transporting infants, winnowing acorns, and so on. Acorn mush and other foodstuffs were cooked in tightly-woven baskets, filled with water, into which hot stones were placed.

Clam shell disc beads and olivella shell beads were traded to the Miwok by tribes to the west, north and northwest. Strings of these beads were considered a sign of great wealth.

Present Status It was the tragedy of the Sierra Miwok that the principal gold-bearing regions of California lay within their territory. The effect of the Gold Rush was that the Southern Sierra Miwok were reduced from an estimated 2,000 to 3,000 individuals in 1850, to less than 200 in 1900. Today, many people of Miwok descent live throughout the world; some continue to adhere to aspects of their people's culture, hoping to keep it alive for future Miwok descendants.

ACKNOWLEDGMENTS

We would like to thank the staff of the National Park Service in Yosemite, particularly Craig Bates, for its help in developing this book. Craig shared his extensive knowledge of the Southern Sierra Miwok, and was always willing to review both text and illustrations. Thanks, also, to Pat Wight for introducing us to this project.

RELATED READINGS

Barrett, Samuel A., and Edward W. Gifford. "Miwok Material Culture." *Bulletin of the Public Museum of the City of Milwaukee* 2 (March 1933): 119-137. (Reprinted as *Indian Life of the Yosemite Region* by the Yosemite Association.)

Bates, Craig. D. *The Miwok in Yosemite—Southern Miwok Life, History, and Language in the Yosemite Region.* Yosemite National Park: Yosemite Association, 1996.

Bates, Craig D., and Martha J. Lee. *Tradition and Innovation: A Basket History of the Indians of the Yosemite-Mono Lake Area.* YosemiteNational Park: Yosemite Association, 1990.

Bunnell, Lafayette Houghton. *Discovery of the Yosemite and the Indian War of 1851 Which Led to That Event,* 4th ed. Los Angeles: G.W. Gerlicher, 1911. (Reprinted by the Yosemite Association in 1991.)

Culin, Stewart. *Games of the North American Indians.* New York: Dover Publications, Inc., 1975. Unabridged republication of the Accompanying Paper, "Games of the North American Indians," from the *Twenty-Fourth Annual Report of the Bureau of American Ethnology to the Smithsonian Institution, 1902-1903,* originally published by the Government Printing Office in 1907.

Gendar, Jeannine. *Grass Games and Moon Races.* Berkeley, CA: Heyday Books, 1995.

Gifford, Edward W., and Gwendoline Harris Block, compilers. *Californian Indian Nights' Entertainment: Stories of the Creation of the World, of Man, of Fire, of the Sun, of Thunder, etc.; of Coyote, the Land of the Dead, the Sky Land, Monsters, Animal People, etc.* Glendale, CA: Arthur H. Clark Company, 1930. (Reprinted by the University of Nebraska Press as a Bison Book in 1990.)

Godfrey, Elizabeth. *Yosemite Indians.* Yosemite National Park: Yosemite Association, 1941, 1973; revised edition, 1977.

Heizer, Robert F., and Albert B. Elsasser. *The Natural World of the California Indians: California Natural History Guides, No. 46.* Berkeley and Los Angeles: University of California Press, 1980.

Hinton, Leanne. *Flutes of Fire: Essays on California Indian Languages.* Berkeley, CA: Heyday Books, 1994.

La Pena, Frank, Craig D. Bates, and Steven P. Medley, compilers. *Legends of the Yosemite Miwok.* Yosemite National Park: Yosemite Association, 1981, 1993.

Merriam, C. Hart. *Dawn of the World: Weird Tales of the Mewan Indians of California.* Cleveland: Arthur H. Clark Company, 1910. (Reprinted by the University of Nebraska Press as a Bison Book in 1993.)

Ortiz, Bev. *It Will Live Forever: Traditional Yosemite Indian Acorn Preparation.* Berkeley, CA: Heyday Books, 1991.

Powers, Stephen. *Tribes of California.* Berkeley and Los Angeles: University of California Press, 1976. Reprinted from *Contributions to North American Ethnology, Volume III, Department of the Interior, U.S. Geographical and Geological Survey of the Rocky Mountain Region, J.W. Powell, in charge* (Washington, DC: Government Printing Office, 1877).

Rawls, James J. *Indians of California: The Changing Image.* Norman, OK: University of Oklahoma Press, 1984.

INTERNET RESOURCES

Miwok Bibliography — www.mip.berkeley.edu/cilc/bibs/miwok.html

The Miwok Indians of Yosemite — mariposa.yosemite.net/woodland/miwok.htm

Yosemite Bookstore — www.yosemitestore.com

Yosemite National Park Web Site — www.nps.gov/yose/yo_visit.htm

Miwok Resources — www.qal.berkeley.edu/~kroeber/iup.ca.ind/miwok.frames.html

Yosemite Teacher Resources — www.nps.gov/yose/teach.htm